THE BLOB

BY IAN THORNE
BASED ON JACK H. HARRIS PRODUCTION OF THE BLOB
FROM THE MOTION PICTURE STARRING STEVE McQUEEN

EDITED BY
DR. HOWARD SCHROEDER
Professor in Reading and Language Arts
Dept. of Elementary Education
Mankato State University

Library of Congress Catalog Card Number: 81-19633

International Standard Book Numbers:
0-89686-212-7 Library Bound
0-89686-215-1 Paperback

Design - Tammy Loe

Library of Congress Cataloging in Publication Data

Thorne, Ian.
  The blob.

  (Monster series)
  SUMMARY: When a meteor crashes to earth, it carries a mysterious destructive
blob inside.
  (1. Science fiction) I. Schroeder, Howard. II. Title. III. Series: Thorne, Ian.
Monster series.
PZ7.T3927Bl   (Fic)   81-19633
ISBN 0-89686-212-7 (lib. bdg.)   AACR2
ISBN 0-89686-215-1 (pbk.)

PHOTOGRAPHIC CREDITS

Worldwide Entertainment Corp: Cover, 2, 6, 9, 10-11, 13, 14, 15, 16-17, 20-21,
22-23, 24-25, 26-27, 28, 31, 34, 36-37, 38, 40, 41, 42, 43, 44-45, 46
Forrest J. Ackerman: 19, 33

Published by
CRESTWOOD HOUSE, INC.
Highway 66 South
P.O. Box 3427
Mankato, MN 56002-3427

Printed in the United States of America

THE BLOB

BY IAN THORNE
BASED ON JACK H. HARRIS PRODUCTION OF THE BLOB
FROM THE MOTION PICTURE STARRING STEVE McQUEEN

THE METEOR

Young Steve Andrews was proud of his car. Even though it was an older car, he had worked on the engine until it sang. The paint job sparkled like new and the inside was spotless.

"Let's go for a ride," he said to his friend, Jane Martin. "It's a nice night."

"All right," she said, "if you promise not to get cute." Jane smiled at him.

"I am never cute!" Steve protested. "I'm

Steve Andrews (Steve McQueen) asks Jane Martin (Aneta Corseaut) to go for a ride. "All right," she said, "if you promise not to get cute."

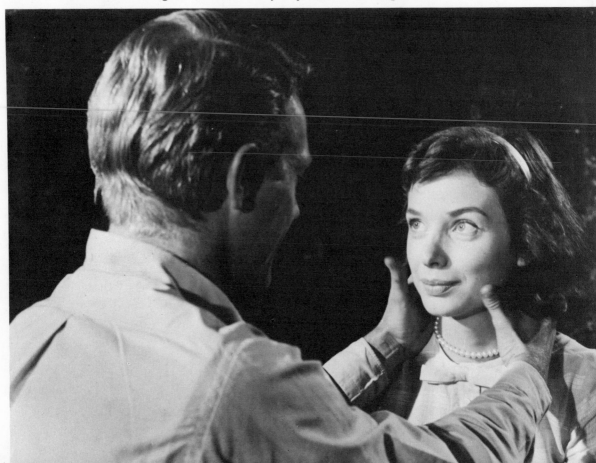

adorable!"

Jane laughed. She climbed into the car beside Steve and they drove away. The engine roared as Steve opened it up outside town. The car seemed to fly along under the starry sky.

"Look!" cried Jane. "A meteor! A shooting star!" She made Steve stop the car so they could watch the streaks of light. There seemed to be a great many meteors falling that night.

Suddenly a huge meteor burst into sight. It hissed and seemed to fall behind some nearby trees. "I think I heard it crash," Steve exclaimed. "It was close by. Come on, let's see if we can find it!"

He started the car and pulled back onto the road, tires screeching.

"Hold on, Jane! We're racing for a star tonight! If we find it, the whole town will envy us."

Still laughing, they sped away.

Meanwhile, in the deep woods nearby, a dog was barking madly outside a tumbledown shack.

"Hush up, Bozo!" yelled a voice from inside. But the dog kept on barking.

"Hush up, I say!" Old Barney came to the door and opened it. The dog rushed inside, whimpering. Barney was puzzled. He squinted into the dark woods. Was there a strange light back in among the trees? A fire, maybe?

He cocked his head and listened. A strange hissing sound could be heard. Muttering, Barney got a lantern and went off into the forest.

Not far from the shack he found a hole in the ground. It was fresh. And there was smoke rising from it.

"Well, what have we here?" Barney asked himself.

He took a stick and poked at an object down in the bottom of the hole. The thing fell open like a cracked egg, and inside was . . . a blob.

"Doggone!" said Barney. He jabbed the soft mass with the stick. The blob clung to the wood. It wrapped itself around the stick and swiftly oozed up it. In an instant, it attached itself to Barney's hand. The old man screamed.

Steve and Jane were driving on a nearby road.

"I could have sworn the meteor landed just over this hill," Steve said.

Suddenly a dark form moved in the headlights. Jane cried, "Steve, watch out!"

Steve hit the brakes. "It looked like a man. I don't think we hit him." He flung the door open and got out of the car to take a look. He found Barney lying in the road, weeping and mumbling.

"Are you hurt?" Steve asked anxiously.

"Take me to a doctor!" the old man groaned. "I can't get it off. I can't get it off!"

He held up his hand with the terrible blob clinging to it. The thing was slimy and shining and it had a fearsome smell. Steve and Jane gasped.

"Help him into the car," Jane said. She told Barney, "We'll take you to Doc Hallen right away."

The old man collapsed on the car seat. Spinning the hot rod's tires, Steve floored the pedal. They roared back to town.

Steve and Jane get Old Barney to Doc Hallen's.

At Dr. Hallen's house, Steve and Jane tried to explain what had happened.

"We picked the old man up on the road, Doc," said Steve. "He's got this funny thing on his hand."

The doctor examined Barney. Jane whispered to

Dr. Hallen examines the old man.

Steve, "Look! The thing's gotten bigger! Now it's all over his arm."

"I'll take care of you, old-timer," Dr. Hallen told Barney. He gave him medicine for the pain.

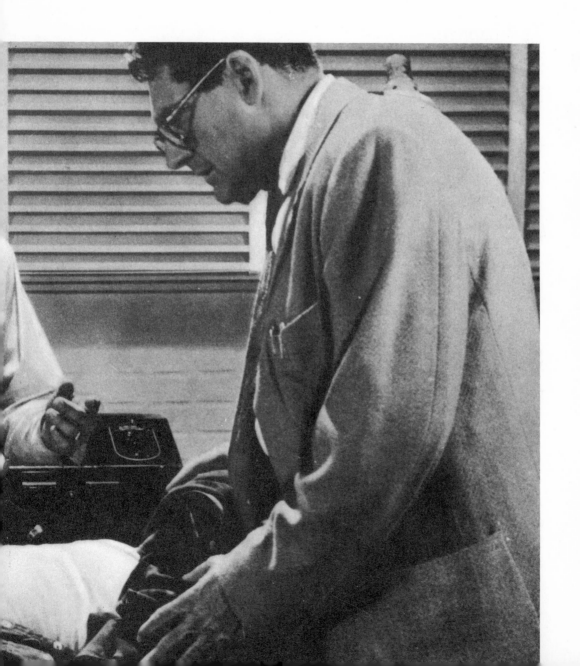

"What is that thing on his arm?" Steve asked.

"I don't know," the doctor replied. "I'll try to find out. You two might be able to help me."

"Sure, Doc!" said Steve. "What can we do?"

"Go out to the place where you found him," said Hallen. "See if you can find somebody who knows what happened."

"Right!" said Steve. He and Jane left the doctor's house. Outside, standing next to Steve's car, they found three friends — Al, Tony, and Mooch.

"Hey, here he comes!" Mooch exclaimed. "The stock-car racing champ of Kingman County!"

"We saw you come burning into town, man," said Al. "Good thing Sergeant Burt isn't on patrol tonight."

"I got my hot rod ready and waiting, champ," Tony said. "Let's drag!"

"I've got to do something for Doc Hallen," Steve told them. "He wants me to check on some people out on the North Road."

"Hey, we wanted you to go with us to the midnight spook show at the Grand," said Mooch.

"Listen," Steve said. "You guys come with us. It won't take long. Then we'll catch the movie together."

"Okay," the three boys agreed. They piled into Tony's hot rod. The two cars sped away.

Back inside the house, Dr. Hallen was very worried. He phoned his nurse. "Can you come right away, Kate? An emergency. Old Barney is here and has some kind of growth on his arm. I may have to amputate . . ."

Steve and Jane meet Al, Mooch and Tony.

Steve finds a mysterious hollow meteorite.

The five teenagers drove to the place where Steve and Jane had picked up old Barney. They got out of their cars and searched the woods. It was a lonely place. They found the strange hole in the ground that the meteor had made when it fell.

"Hey! Somebody left a lantern here!" said Tony. He picked up Barney's lantern and peered into the hole. "Something down there."

Steve picked up the pieces of the hollow meteor. "We saw a shooting star about an hour ago. Maybe this is it!"

"Wow!" exclaimed Tony. "This little rock might have been hot-rodding around the universe!"

Suddenly they were aware of a dog barking.

"I'll bet there's a house close by," said Jane. "Let's go look. The people might know something."

The five of them hurried through the woods and came to Barney's shack. The little dog, Bozo, was shut up inside. He barked wildly.

"Anybody home?" Steve called. But no one answered. "This must be Barney's place."

"We can't leave the dog locked up," Jane said. "Let's take him with us back to town."

"Okay," Steve agreed.

Jane takes charge of the old man's dog.

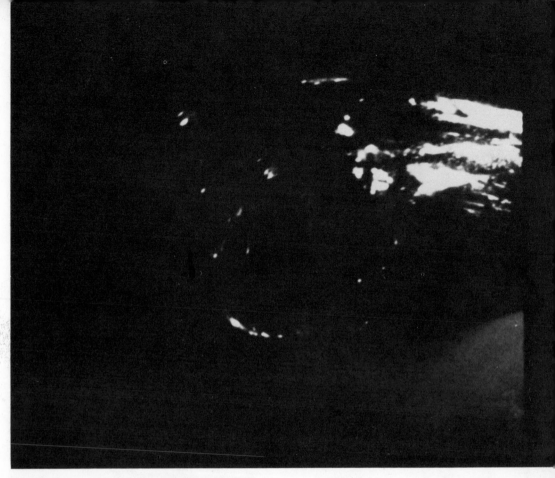

Dr. Hallen's office is invaded by the blob.

THE BLOB AT LARGE

Meanwhile, Dr. Hallen's nurse arrived at his home. "I'm afraid we'll have to operate, Kate," the doctor said. "But don't touch that thing on his arm. It seems to be feeding on his flesh."

Kate nodded grimly. She went into the examining room. But no one was there! "Doctor? Where is the patient?" Kate called. And then she screamed.

Slithering over the floor was a slimy mass. It was the blob. Alive. And coming after her.

"Stand still, Kate!" Dr. Hallen shouted. "Get that acid from the cabinet behind you! Throw it at the

thing!"

Kate splashed acid on the blob. But it was not harmed. "I'll get my gun!" said Hallen.

"Don't leave me here with it!" Kate pleaded. But the doctor was gone. "Come back!" she cried.

The blob came closer. Kate screamed and screamed.

When Dr. Hallen returned, Kate had vanished. He saw only the blob. He fired at the thing, but bullets didn't hurt it. Nothing seemed to hurt it.

Dr. Hallen turned and fled . . .

At that moment, Steve's car pulled up outside. "You stay here," he told Jane. "I'll tell Doc what we found."

He went up to the house. It seemed that no one was home. "That's funny," Steve said. "I wonder —"

From inside the house came the sound of terrible screams. The blinds at the window rattled. Hands were pulling at the blinds, trying to open the window. And then the hands disappeared. The screaming stopped.

"Steve! Steve!" called Jane from the car. "What's happening?"

Steve looked in the window. His eyes widened with shock and horror. He turned and ran to the car.

"What is it?" Jane asked.

Steve whispered, "It got Doc Hallen. The thing. Just like the blob on the old man's hand, only bigger. It pulled him down. And then it was on his head. And in just a second or two — he disappeared."

"What — !" cried Jane. "Disappeared?"

"Doc disappeared. The blob seemed to absorb him!"

"What are we going to do?" Jane asked.

Steve got into the car. "There's only one thing we can do. Go to the police."

But when Steve and Jane got to the police station, they could not get the officers to believe them.

"A monster?" scoffed Sgt. Burt. "Oh, come on."

"It's true," Steve said. "This blobby thing was all over Doc Hallen and it killed him."

"You kids!" said the sergeant. "First it's drag racing all over town, and now man-eating goo!"

"We're telling the truth!" Steve protested.

Lieutenant Dave Barton said, "We're going to have to check this out."

"If this is a gag, you kids won't do much laughing!" Burt said to Steve.

Sgt. Burt and Lt. Dave Barton listen to Steve's story.

The two policemen, Steve, and Jane drove to Dr. Hallen's house. The place seemed deserted.

"It might still be inside," Steve warned. "Be careful."

"Don't you worry about us, kid," said Sgt. Burt laughing. He knocked. When there was no answer, he went inside. Steve and Jane followed the police.

They came into the examining room and found only broken glass. The door to Dr. Hallen's den, where he kept his gun, was locked.

"He was in there when I saw the blob get him," Steve said.

Not a sign of the blob!

Sgt. Burt went outside and entered the den through the window. He unlocked the door and the others came in. "Just look at this mess!" said Burt. "But no mysterious blob."

"It must have gotten away," said Steve.

The sergeant glared at the boy. "Oh, yeah? Let me tell you what happened here tonight. You broke in here. You messed up the place. Then you rigged the door so it would lock and came to feed us your story. This whole stunt was a put-up job, just to make us look silly! Well, it's not funny!"

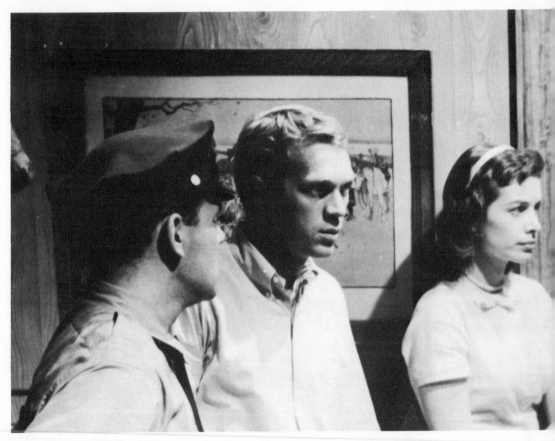

Mrs. Porter casts doubt on Steve's story.

Just then a woman came into Dr. Hallen's house. It was Mrs. Porter, the doctor's housekeeper.

"What's going on here?" she exclaimed. "Oh, my! Just wait till the doctor gets back and sees this!"

"Back?" said Dave Barton. "Back from where?"

"He went to a convention," said Mrs. Porter. "He told me to keep an eye on the place."

"But that's not true," Steve protested. "He was here this evening. We brought in an old man with a blob on his hand, and Doc said he'd take care of him."

"An old man, huh?" snarled Sgt. Burt. "Where is

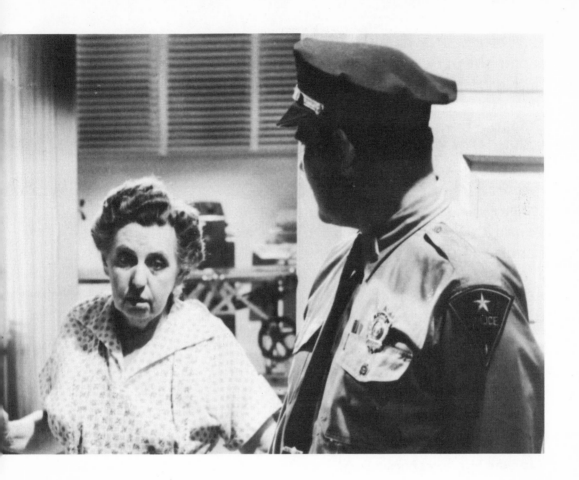

he, then?"

"The blob . . . must have gotten him, too," said Steve.

Dave Barton found the doctor's gun on the floor. Several bullets had been fired from it. But there were no bullet holes to be found.

"This is serious business," Sgt. Burt said. "We'll check this for prints."

"You won't find mine," Steve insisted.

"We'll see about that down at the station," said Burt. "You kids are under arrest."

A block or two away, in a neighborhood auto repair shop, two men were working late.

"Hey, Marty," called one man from beneath a car. "Hand me that small hammer, will you?"

Marty bent down with the tool. "Here you go, Willis." He turned back to his own work. "Why don't we quit for the night? We can finish tomorrow."

"Nope," said Willis from under the car. "I'm not gonna be here tomorrow." There was a sound of hammering.

Marty was busy with his own work. He did not notice that something very strange was oozing under the garage door . . .

"Where you going, Willis?" asked Marty.

"Hunting. Hey, come along. We'll have a lot of fun."

The harsh light of the garage shone on the blob. It crept under the door as easily as a puddle of soup.

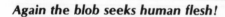

Again the blob seeks human flesh!

Then it seemed to gather itself into a flowing lump. It moved toward the car that Willis was working on.

"I'd like to go hunting," Marty said. "But I don't think my wife would like it."

"Tell her you've got a sick friend!" Willis said.

Marty wiped his hands and got ready to go home. "Some other time, Willis. Good night." He put on his jacket and left the garage. He did not notice the mass of slime that lurked in the shadows.

"Hey, Marty? You still there?" Willis called.

The blob moved swiftly over the floor now. It reached the car where Willis lay flat on his back, still hammering.

"What the heck — !" the man exclaimed. The hammering noise stopped. There was a sudden clang as the tool fell to the concrete floor. And then came an eerie, bubbling yell.

The yelling went on for a few minutes. After that the garage was very silent.

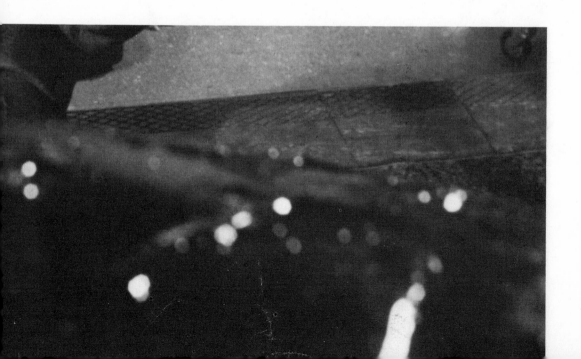

The fathers of Steve and Jane meet their children in the police station.

THE BLOB GROWS

Lt. Dave Barton was trying to be patient. "Look, Steve. All we want to do is clear up this mess. But you keep telling me about a monster."

"You've known me for a long time," Steve said. "Would I do a thing like tearing up Doc's house?"

"I don't think you would, but — "

"Would Jane go along with a silly prank?" Steve asked. "You know better."

The policeman shook his head. Just then, two men entered the station. They were Jane's father, Mr. Martin, and Steve's father, Mr. Andrews.

Mr. Martin said to Steve, "Young man, this is the last time you'll ever take my daughter out!"

"Steve didn't do anything wrong," Jane said.

Mr. Andrews looked sadly at his son. "Can you explain this, Steve?"

"We saw something terrible tonight, Dad," Steve said. "But nobody will believe us!"

Lt. Dave Barton said, "I think the best thing now is for all of you to go home and get some sleep. We'll make sense of this tomorrow."

Steve and Jane went home. But they didn't go to sleep. They could not sleep, knowing the blob was loose!

Jane crept out of her bed as soon as the house was dark and phoned Steve. She met her little brother, Danny, on the stairs.

"Where you going, Jane?" asked Danny.

"Shh," she said. "I have something important to do. But it's a secret. You stay here and guard the house."

"Okay," said Danny.

Jane met Steve outside. "What are we going to do?" she asked him.

"I don't know," he replied. "I'm beginning to think that we dreamed the whole thing."

"Oh, Steve," said Jane.

He shook his head. "Plenty of people — ordinary people — think they see things. And then — well, they find they were mistaken. But it seemed so real! I know I saw that thing get Doc Hallen! I did, Jane."

"I believe you," she said.

"If that blob is real, then it's out there right now. In our town. It could be killing more people. Somehow, we have to do something. Give a warning. Maybe even find the blob and then show it to the police so they'll believe us! But just the two of us —"

"We could get somebody to help us," Jane suggested. "Your three friends. Tony, Mooch, and Al."

Steve nodded. His eyes sparkled. "They're at the midnight horror movie. Let's go get them!"

The two of them got into Steve's car and drove to the theatre.

Steve and Jane must do something about the blob.

Steve and Jane found the three boys in the balcony of the theatre with their girl friends. They did not want to leave the movie.

"Hey! We paid good money to see this!" Mooch complained. "If we leave, I'm out my money!"

"There's a real monster prowling this town," Steve told him. "We're the only ones who can warn people."

The other teenagers laughed at first. But Steve told them about the horrible thing he had seen at Doc Hallen's house.

"I think it was inside that hollow meteor we found," Steve said. "It feeds on human flesh. It could wipe out the whole town! The police won't believe that it's real either. It's up to us to spread the word — and maybe find the thing. Some of you go around knocking on doors, and the rest spread out and keep your eyes open."

Finally, the teenagers agreed to do as Steve asked. They tried to tell people that a terrible monster was loose in town.

Not a single person would believe the warning.

Steve and Jane drove along the main street of town, past the supermarket owned by Steve's father.

"Look there!" exclaimed Jane. "In the doorway of the market. It's the old man's little dog that ran away from us back at Doc Hallen's place. Let's take the poor thing with us."

Steve stopped the car and they got out. When they went for the dog, they discovered that the market door was open.

"That's strange," Steve said. "We better check this out."

It was dark inside the market. There was no sign of

the janitor who was supposed to be cleaning.

Jane hugged the dog, which was whimpering.

"What's wrong?" she asked the little animal.

And suddenly she saw what was wrong. Something slimy was moving in the shadows. Something alive.

Jane screamed. She turned to run and crashed into a stack of canned goods. She fell and the dog ran away, yelping.

The blob flowed across the floor toward her.

The blob is prowling the supermarket!

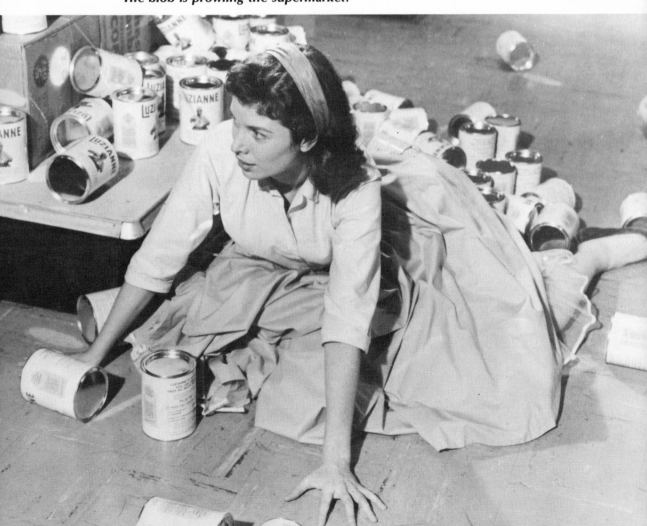

"Jane! What's the matter?" cried Steve.

"It's here!" she sobbed. "The blob!"

Steve grabbed Jane from the floor and carried her away. The two of them began to run with the slimy monster flowing swiftly after them.

They raced into the meat department. Steve picked up a sharp cleaver and threw it at the blob. But the sharp steel only sank into the gooey mass, doing no harm. The blob kept on coming, faster and faster!

There was only one place to hide. The meat locker had a heavy door. Not even the blob would be able to get them in there. Steve pulled Jane after him into the meat locker and slammed the door shut.

Jane was crying. "Oh, Steve! What are we going to do?"

Through the thick door came the sound of a dog barking. And then the barking stopped. Jane moaned. "Oh, the poor little dog . . ."

Steve and Jane take refuge in the freezer.

32

"What are we going to do, Steve?"

But Steve was not thinking of the dog. He looked at the bottom of the door. Something was oozing through the thin crack where the door met the floor.

Steve pulled Jane deep into the locker. Sides of beef hung around them. It was very cold and the two teenagers shivered. Jane sobbed and hid her face.

"Nothing can stop that thing!" Steve muttered.

But he was wrong.

As it flowed over the cold floor, the blob slowed down. It stopped. A miracle seemed to occur when it began to flow backwards instead of forwards. It oozed back under the door and left Steve and Jane alone.

A few moments passed before Steve and Jane realized what had happened. They were safe!

"Do you suppose it's really gone?" Jane asked fearfully.

"I don't know. But we've got to get out of here. If we stay here, we'll freeze. Come on."

He opened the meat locker door very carefully. Outside, the deserted supermarket was very quiet. There was no sign of the blob.

"Let's go!" Steve cried.

He and Jane raced down the aisle toward the front door. They fled into the street and found their teen-age friends standing outside.

"Hey, where you guys been?" Tony asked.

"We found the blob," Steve said grimly. "It was inside. I think it got the janitor."

"And that little dog we found," Jane added tearfully.

Mooch laughed. "The old man's dog? Naw, he's okay. I saw him running down the street. Scared stiff."

Jane smiled her relief.

"What do we do now?" asked Tony.

"We're going to wake this town up," Steve exclaimed, "and make it listen to us!"

Steve tells townspeople about the blob.

THE TOWN VS. THE BLOB

"Everybody to your cars!" Steve ordered. "We need noisemakers. Horns. Whistles. Set off all the fire alarms! Mooch, you go ring the church bell! I'll wind up the old air raid siren on top of the town hall! Honk your car horns! Do anything you can to make the biggest racket this town's ever heard!"

The teenagers scattered. They met other young people coming out of the movie and got them to help. A few minutes later, the noise started.

It was like New Year's Eve in the middle of summer.

All over town, the lights began to go on. Steve's parents woke and found that he was gone. Jane's parents discovered that their daughter was not in bed, and their young son, Danny, was gone, too.

"Has the town gone mad?" Mr. Martin asked. "I'll get to the bottom of this." He ran for his car and drove to the center of town. There a crowd was gathered in front of the supermarket listening to young Steve Andrews.

"We had to make this noise," Steve was saying. "It was the only way to make you listen to us."

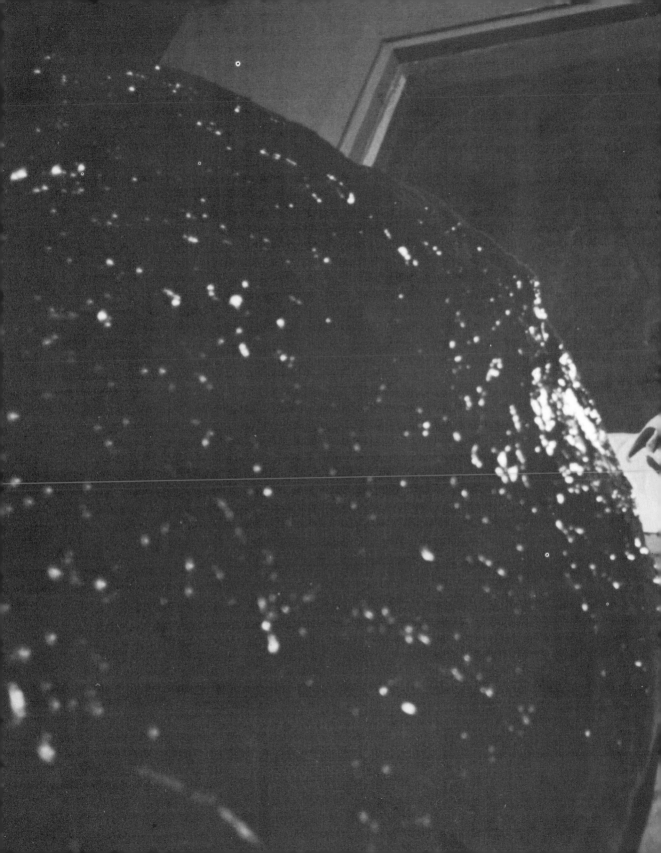

At that very moment, the blob was striking again!

The slimy monster had crept out of the market and flowed away down a dark alley. It came to the movie theatre and sensed that there were people still inside. It flowed in under the closed door, oozed across the lobby, and went into the dark booth where the projectionist was showing another horror movie.

Before the man could utter a sound, the blob surged up. It covered the man's body with deadly slime.

Within a few seconds, the blob had grown much larger. There was not a trace of the projectionist.

The blob was not satisfied. It was hungrier than ever! It oozed out of the projection booth into the theatre. A real horror took the place of the one on the screen. The crowd panicked. Screams filled the dark theatre as the blob found victim after victim.

The people who escaped ran into the street. They fled from the pursuing blob. Now the slimy monster had grown to enormous size. It flowed toward the supermarket, where a large crowd stood in the street.

"Run! Run!" the fleeing people shouted. "The monster is coming!"

The blob flows toward the projectionist.

The people scattered in all directions. Danny, Jane's little brother, ran into a nearby diner. Steve and Jane saw him and followed after.

"Hey! What's happening?" asked George, the diner's owner. The waitress, Sally, looked outside and saw the blob coming. She screamed.

"Quick!" shouted Steve. "Everybody out the back!"

But it was too late to escape. The gigantic blob flowed over the entire diner just as George slammed the door and locked it.

"It's all over us!" Steve said. "We're finished."

The diner's phone rang.

The blob engulfs the diner just as Steve gets inside.

Lt. Dave Barton phones Steve inside the diner.

Steve picked up the phone. It was Lt. Dave Barton of the police.

"We're going to drop a power line on that thing," Dave said. "Maybe we can burn it up. All of you get down into the diner's cellar."

The police outside cut a high voltage line so that it fell on the blob. Electric sparks sizzled. Smoke billowed up. The diner was catching on fire — but the deadly blob seemed unharmed. It began to flow inside the burning diner.

"We found a way to stop the blob!"

Down in the diner's cellar, the trapped people faced two kinds of death: fire and the blob!

Steve grabbed up a CO_2 fire extinguisher. He squirted it at the flames. Some of the icy cold gas from the extinguisher hit the approaching blob. The monster shrank back. It flowed away from the CO_2.

"It's afraid of the cold," Steve said. "Look! Just like in the meat locker! It can't stand cold. That's the way to attack it."

He ran back upstairs with the others following. Quickly, he grabbed the phone. Dave was still on the line, trying to find out what had happened.

"Dave!" cried Steve. "We found a way to stop the blob! CO_2 fire extinguishers! It can't stand cold!"

"Alright!" Dave said. He looked at the crowd gathered around his police car. "Where can we get fire extinguishers?"

Mr. Martin said, "At the high school. We must have twenty of them."

"What are we waiting for?" yelled Tony, Al, and Mooch. They and the other teenagers piled into their cars. They roared off to the school and got the extinguishers.

The teenagers hurry to obtain fire extinguishers.

The teenagers and the firemen began to attack the blob. They sprayed the slimy mass with cold CO_2 gas. Clouds of vapor rose.

The blob's slime seemed to be freezing solid. It fell from the diner's roof and lay shuddering in the street.

Cold gas from the extinguishers freezes the blob.

The boys and the firemen poured on more CO_2. The blob was hardly moving now. Long before the extinguishers ran out of CO_2, the terrible blob lay quiet.

Frozen stiff.

Steve, Jane and Danny came running out of the diner. Their parents met them and hugged them. Then Steve hugged Jane.

Dave Barton said, "Thanks to Steve, we were able to stop this monster. The whole town owes this boy a vote of thanks."

The crowd cheered.

"I'm glad you finally believed me," Steve said.

"We'll never doubt your word again, son," said Mr. Martin.

The little dog came racing through the crowd and stood barking in front of Steve, Jane, and Danny.

"I'm going to keep him," Danny said.

Jane's family is reunited.

THE END OF THE BLOB

But what was to be done with the frozen blob?

Dave Barton called up Washington and talked to people in the Pentagon. "We've got this thing under control," he said. "But we won't rest easy until it's frozen solid."

"It might be better to blow it up," said the man at the Pentagon.

"You can't do that," Dave protested. "That would only spread the thing all over! Each little piece would grow into another blob!"

"Well — what do you think we should do?" asked the Pentagon man.

Dave said, "Send us the biggest transport plane that the Air Force has. Load this thing inside and keep it frozen. Then fly it up to the Arctic! Drop it someplace where it'll never thaw out."

The man at the Pentagon promised to send a plane at once. David smiled with relief. He hung up the phone.

"Well, folks," he told the crowd, "that's that. The Air Force is coming for the blob."

"But it's not dead," Jane said softly. "Is it?"

"No," Dave said. "But we've stopped it."

Steve looked at the frozen thing. "At least — for as long as the Arctic stays cold."

MONSTERS

> I SUGGEST YOU READ ABOUT MY FRIENDS!

THE BLOB
DRACULA
GODZILLA
KING KONG
THE MUMMY
FRANKENSTEIN
MAD SCIENTISTS
THE WOLF MAN
THE DEADLY MANTIS
IT CAME FROM OUTER SPACE
FRANKENSTEIN MEETS WOLFMAN
CREATURE FROM THE BLACK LAGOON

CRESTWOOD HOUSE

P.O. BOX 3427 MANKATO, MINNESOTA 56002-3427
Write Us for a Complete Catalog